P9-EEB-742

GOOD DOG

4 Books in 1!

Home Is Where the Heart Is
Raised in a Barn
Herd You Loud and Clear
Fireworks Night

by Cam Higgins

illustrated by Ariel Landy

LITTLE SIMON

New York London Toronto Sydney New Delhi

This book is a work of fiction. Any references to historical events, real people, or real places are used fictitiously. Other names, characters, places, and events are products of the author's imagination, and any resemblance to actual events or places or persons, living or dead, is entirely coincidental.

LITTLE SIMON
An imprint of Simon & Schuster Children's Publishing Division
New York   London   Toronto   Sydney   New Delhi
1230 Avenue of the Americas, New York, New York 10020
This Little Simon hardcover edition June 2021
Home Is Where the Heart Is, *Raised in a Barn*, and
Herd You Loud and Clear copyright © 2020 by Simon & Schuster, Inc.
Fireworks Night copyright © 2021 by Simon & Schuster, Inc.
All rights reserved, including the right of reproduction
in whole or in part in any form.
LITTLE SIMON is a registered trademark of Simon & Schuster, Inc.,
and associated colophon is a trademark of Simon & Schuster, Inc.
For information about special discounts for bulk purchases,
please contact Simon & Schuster Special Sales at 1-866-506-1949
or business@simonandschuster.com.
The Simon & Schuster Speakers Bureau
can bring authors to your live event.
For more information or to book an event contact
the Simon & Schuster Speakers Bureau at 1-866-248-3049
or visit our website at www.simonspeakers.com.
Series designed by Leslie Mechanic
Manufactured in the United States of America 0722 FFG
4 6 8 10 9 7 5 3
Library of Congress Control Number 2021936176
ISBN 978-1-6659-0706-4
ISBN 978-1-5344-7902-9 (*Home Is Where the Heart Is* ebook)
ISBN 978-1-5344-7905-0 (*Raised in a Barn* ebook)
ISBN 978-1-5344-7908-1 (*Herd You Loud and Clear* ebook)
ISBN 978-1-5344-9533-3 (*Fireworks Night* ebook)
These titles were previously published individually
in hardcover and paperback by Little Simon.

Home Is Where the Heart Is

Home Is Where the Heart Is

Raised in a Barn

Raised in a Barn

Herd You Loud and Clear

Herd You Loud and Clear

Fireworks Night

Fireworks Night

GOOD D🐾G

1

Home Is Where the Heart Is

CONTENTS

CHAPTER 1: THE MUD BATH   7

CHAPTER 2: BARN CATS   23

CHAPTER 3: LOST TAG   33

CHAPTER 4: ULTRA-DOGGY-ALARM   47

CHAPTER 5: A GAME OF CHICKEN   59

CHAPTER 6: COUNTING SHEEP   73

CHAPTER 7: SCRAPPER   85

CHAPTER 8: KING AND DIVA   95

CHAPTER 9: THE UP-UPSTAIRS   103

CHAPTER 10: HOME IS WHERE THE HEART IS   117

The
Mud Bath

Mud.

Is there anything better than the cool feeling of it against your fur or the way it squishy-oozes between your paws?

And the smell! The sweet perfume of grass and springtime and earth. There is nothing like fresh mud.

Of course, I know I shouldn't have rolled around in mud, but that morning was special.

It had rained for the past three entire days on the Davis farm, which meant I was stuck in the house.

Being inside wasn't the worst thing in the world because I got to spend time with my human family.

Jennica and Darnell are my human mom and dad. They make great lap pillows, scratch behind my ears, and like to play fetch.

I've even trained them to give me leftovers when I've been good.

They say, "Good dog, Bo," because
that's my name, and then they scrape
yummy scraps into my food bowl.

I also have a human sister and brother, Imani and Wyatt. We are best friends, and we share everything!

Beds.

Socks.

Sticks.

Well, okay, maybe not sticks. I think sticks are the best.

What else is chewy on the inside and crunchy on the outside? I try to share them with Imani and Wyatt, but they keep throwing them away no matter how many times I bring them back.

Humans are funny like that.

Staying inside was fine when it rained for so long, but I'm more of an outside dog.

I like to spend my days exploring the farm and visiting my animal friends.

There's Star and Grey and their foal, Comet. She loves to chase me around. One day she might even catch me!

There's also a head hen named Clucks.

And there's a head
rooster named Rufus.
They're nice, even if
they peck at my feet
when I come near.

Nanny Sheep always reminds me
not to scare Clucks and Rufus. They
get jumpy around dogs, I guess.

And then there's Zonks. He's my pig pal.

Which brings me back to the mud. As soon as I saw the sunshine and clear skies that morning, I dashed out the front door before Imani and Wyatt could even put on their boots.

I went straight to the pigpen.

"Hi, Bo," Zonks oinked as he tumbled in the mud.

I stopped and admired the mess. "Wow! It's so . . . dirty!"

That made Zonks smile. "Some animals love rain because it brings rainbows, but not me. I love rain because it brings mud!"

"Can I try?" I asked.

Zonks plopped onto his back and waved with his hoof. "Come on in."

I stepped forward, and my paw sank into the gooey mud. I couldn't help myself. This was going to be fun.

I flopped onto my back and rolled all around. The mud covered my fur like a cool, soft blanket.

"Bo! Where are you, boy?" It was Imani calling me. I should have run to her, but I was in mud heaven.

Wyatt reached the pigpen first. He stared at me and shook his head.

Then Imani joined him at the fence and moaned, "Good grief, Bo!"

I gave a playful bark to invite them in.

But humans don't always understand Dog.

And from the looks on their faces, I don't think humans will *ever* understand mud.

Barn Cats

Here's a secret: I trust Imani and Wyatt.

They may not love mud as much as I do yet, but they know what's best for a pup like me.

So when they called me, I knew it was time to go.

I said goodbye to Zonks.

Then I said goodbye to the perfect, muddy pigpen and followed the kids back to the house.

Everyone could tell what was coming next. I was headed for the bath.

Baths aren't so bad. I don't mind
them much. But there are some
animals on the farm who do not like
them at all.

Two of those animals are named
King and Diva.

Imani and Wyatt call them barn cats, but I call them *trouble*.

Diva stood on the front porch and hissed when we walked up. "Bo, you poor thing. There's something stuck on your back!"

"What? Where?" I cried.

I wiggled this way and that, trying to see what it could be.

"Oh, Diva, don't you know?" King said with a smirk. "That's just the way dogs always look . . . covered in mud and completely clueless!"

See what I mean? Trouble.

Luckily Wyatt scooted those mean cats away. "Get, you two! You know the rules. Barn cats keep to the barn."

Then he went to run my bath as
Imani plopped me down. We sat
together on the porch.

"You sure love mud, Bo, don't you?"
she asked, scratching behind my ear.

I wagged my tail, and some mud shook loose.

I could hear Diva hiss again in the distance, but Imani just giggled. She has the best giggles!

Hearing her laugh is maybe even better than rolling in mud. *Maybe.*

When the bath was ready, Imani picked me up and brought me inside. She didn't want me to track dirt on the floor.

I thought I was getting too big to be carried, but it felt really nice to be in her arms. Almost as good as mud.

Lost
Tag

Imani set me down in the bathroom.
The tile floor was cold and made me
shiver a little.

"Did you check the water to make
sure it isn't too hot?" Imani asked
Wyatt.

"Yes, Imani," Wyatt said. "I know
how to make a bath for Bo."

I peeked into the tub. There were lots of bubbles and nice smells in the water. It wasn't too deep. Wyatt really does know how to make a nice bath.

He took off my bandanna and my collar, and then I climbed into the tub. I took care not to splash.

The water was warm and nice, and it felt so good. I lay down on my belly so I wouldn't slip.

Wyatt stroked my head and held me gently. Imani reached for the showerhead, turned it on, and let the water fall over me like a soft rain. I closed my eyes and kept still.

"Good boy, Bo," Imani said.

She wet my back and my tail and my tummy. Then Imani and Wyatt rubbed shampoo all over my fur.

I was in doggy heaven!
Even the sudsy
squish sounds
made me
smile, until I
tasted some of
the soap and
yuck!

"Oops, almost over, Bo," said Wyatt as he wiped the bubbles away from my mouth.

When we were done, Imani pulled the drain plug.

I watched the water rush down in a swirl.

Then Imani rinsed me off with the showerhead again.

As the suds ran off my fur, I was a little bit sad to see the mud wash away. But I wasn't too sad. There would be more mud another day.

There is *always* more mud on the farm. We practically grow mud here!

I was squeaky clean now, so Wyatt lifted me out of the tub, and Imani wrapped me in a fluffy blue towel.

Towels are soft and cozy, but they don't always get a pup dry. Imani and Wyatt take such good care of me. The least I could do was help them get the job done.

I *shook shook shook* my whole body, and a spray of water flew in every direction.

Imani and Wyatt squealed and laughed.

Then I ran! The wind would dry me. I darted into Wyatt's bedroom and rolled around on the carpet.

Then I dashed into Imani's room and rolled on her rug.

If you have never rubbed your ears and nose and back on a carpet, you do not know what you are missing. It feels *so* scratchy and good!

A few more shakes and a few more rub-rolls on the ground, and I was good as new, dry as a bone.

Oooh, bones. Yum!

When Wyatt and Imani found me, they were still giggling. I wagged my tail and ran to them.

"You're lucky you're so cute," Imani told me.

She was right. I sure am a lucky pup. And I'm pretty cute . . . if I do say so myself.

Wyatt bent to put my collar on. As he fastened it around my neck, he said, "Huh, your tag is missing."

My tag was *missing*? Oh boy, this sounded like a Bo Davis mystery that needed to be solved!

Ultra–Doggy–Alarm

Wyatt might not be very worried about my missing tag, but I sure was.

There was a time, long ago, when I didn't have a tag of my own.

I don't remember much about the pound, but I remember when the Davis family found me. Imani and Wyatt were much smaller . . . and so was I!

Then they adopted me and brought me home.

They also gave me my special tag. It was shaped like a heart and had my name on one side and my address and phone number on the other. It's supposed to help me if I ever get lost. Luckily, I haven't had to use it.

But I love my tag. It reminds me that I'm part of the Davis family. So if it was missing, I *had* to find it.

The first thing I needed to do was get outside.

Every dog knows the secret to getting outdoors—it's easy.

All you have to do is act like you have to go to the bathroom. It works every time.

You start by standing at the door and scraping your paw on it. Then you look back at your humans.

If that doesn't work, you go over to your people, put your paw on them, and whimper just a little. You have to be careful with the whimpering, though. If you cry too much, your people might think you're hurt or sick and take you to the vet.

If that doesn't work, then it's time to bark your head off and really scratch at the door. Running in circles helps too. I call this move the ultra-doggy-alarm. It's very powerful, so I try to be responsible and save it for when nothing else works.

That morning I only needed to wait by the door, and Wyatt came. But before he let me out, he made me promise not to go back in the mud and get dirty again.

I licked his hand to show I understood. I'd try my very best to stay clean.

The first place I raced to was Zonks's pen.

"Hi, Zonks," I said.

"Hello, Bo," Zonks said. He was still lounging in the mud. Oh, it looked so nice. But no, I reminded myself: I had a mission. There was no time for mud.

"Have you seen my tag?" I asked. "It fell off my collar."

"Well, there was something shiny in the mud," said Zonks. "One of the chicks came by and took it. You know how those chicks love shiny objects."

Oh no, not chickens. Why did it have to be chickens?

5

A Game
of Chicken

Don't get me wrong. Chickens are nice, but I did *not* want to bother the chickens if I didn't have to.

Imani says chickens are just jumpy creatures. I say they're scared of everything.

And the problem is, when they are scared, they are super loud.

Maybe I could sneak into the chicken coop, find my tag, and sneak out without being seen.

I tiptoed quietly over to their pen. Most of the chickens were outside, walking along the far edge of the grass and pecking at the ground.

When it rains, we get more than mud on the farm. The rain also brings out worms.

Chickens *love* worms. In fact, worms might be a chicken's most favorite snack.

So while the flock was hunting for squiggly food, I saw my chance.

I slipped under the fence and into their coop. I saw nests, and inside the nests were eggs. But I did not see my shiny tag.

It was time to get out of there before I was discovered.

I turned to leave when I heard something behind me.

"Hello? *Cluck, cluck.* What are you doing in here? *Cluck, cluck!*"

It was Clucks, the head hen. She's the boss of all the chickens, which means she was also the loudest.

Remember the ultra-doggy-alarm? *Everything* sets off the ultra-*chicky*-alarm for Clucks.

Before I could explain, Clucks began to *bawk* and screech. She flapped her wings and chased me right out of the coop.

But all the other chickens were there in the yard, waiting for me. I was surrounded!

They began clucking and flapping their wings. I might have thought the sky was falling, they were acting so scared.

Suddenly Clucks and Rufus, the head rooster, stepped out of the coop together. The other chickens quieted down.

"*Cluck.* What is the meaning of this, Bo? Why were you in our coop?" Clucks said.

"I'm sorry. I lost my shiny tag this morning when I was visiting Zonks," I explained. "He told me one of your chicks found it."

Rufus waved a wing at the chicks
and nodded to them. Rufus doesn't
speak much—just when he wakes us
up with the sunrise every morning.

A fluffy yellow chick stepped forward and said, "*Cheep, cheep.* I found a shiny thing. I was looking for worms near Zonks's mud, and I saw it. So I was picking it up when Nanny Sheep stopped me. She said the shiny thing did not belong to me."

"*Cluck*, and what did you say to Nanny Sheep?" Clucks asked.

The little chick looked nervous. "Um, I said, 'Finders keepers, I have sharp peepers!' *Cheep*."

The chickens all ruffled their wings and clucked quietly. The other chicks' eyes grew larger than skillets!

Everyone knew Nanny Sheep was the kindest animal on the farm. Only a silly little chick would speak to her so rudely.

"I hope you apologized right away," said Clucks.

All eyes were on the chick.

He looked very ashamed. "I told Nanny Sheep I was sorry. Then I gave her the shiny thing. That's where it is now. I promise! *Cheep!*"

Wow! I was *good* at solving mysteries! I was lucky, too. I'd get to see Nanny Sheep *and* get my tag back.

6

Counting Sheep

Nanny Sheep lived in the field with the other sheep.

Sometimes the cows came out to graze. Now and then the horses came outside to run and munch on hay also. But everyone else must have stayed in the barn, because today I only saw sheep.

I love the sheep. They look like tiny clouds, and their soft wool feels like pillows. But take my word for it: *never* try to nap on them.

Actually, that's how I first met Nanny Sheep.

I was playing fetch in the field and I'd gotten so tired from running, I could hardly keep my eyes open.

So when I found a bale of hay with a mound of the softest, fluffiest cloud piled in front of it, I couldn't help myself. I hopped up onto the hay and leaped into the middle of that cloud.

But the cloud was not as soft as it looked. And it was angry.

In fact, it wasn't a cloud at all. It was a flock of sheep taking a nap. When I landed on top of them, they sprang up and ran away. I fell to the ground.

Sheep do not like being jumped on.
They don't like it one bit.

I told them that I was sorry and
explained that I'd thought they were
a cloud. That just made the sheep
laugh at me.

Nanny Sheep didn't laugh, though.

Instead, she shushed the sheep and made the kindest announcement I had ever heard.

"One day this puppy will grow up to be a big dog, and he will herd us and help the farmers take care of us," Nanny Sheep said. "We should all be friends, and friends do not laugh at each other."

The other sheep stopped laughing, but I started to giggle. I couldn't help it!

"I'm sorry," I woofed. "But actually, it *is* pretty silly that I thought you were a cloud!"

Then everyone laughed again, even Nanny Sheep. The sheep and I have been good friends ever since.

Now I found Nanny Sheep resting in the shade beneath a tree.

"Hello, Bo," she said. "Are you finally here to herd the flock?"

"No, Nanny Sheep, not yet," I said. "I'm looking for something you took from a chick. It's a shiny thing. Do you know it?"

"Oh, yes, I do know it," Nanny Sheep replied. "But I'm afraid I do not have it. It belonged to Blue, and I gave it back to him."

Nanny Sheep looked up and called to Blue. The blue jay flew down from his nest high in the tree and landed next to us.

"Could you tell Bo about your shiny object?" Nanny Sheep asked him.

"The shiny thing you found for me?" Blue said. "It's a small bracelet that the girl gave me. She no longer plays with it."

I sighed.

Blue was telling the truth. Imani loved birds, and she sometimes left tiny toys for Blue on her windowsill.

Blue had lost the bracelet in the rain, but Nanny Sheep returned it.

Well, the mystery of the muddy, shiny thing was solved. But the mystery of my lost tag was not!

Scrapper

On the way back to my house, I heard someone in the woods.

"*Bark*-hey! *Bark*-Bo?"

It was Scrapper, my best dog buddy. He lived next door with the Bryson family.

Scrapper is a small pup, like I am, but his fur is shorter and yellow.

He has a thinner tail that wags when he's happy, and he was born with three legs. Other than that, we are exactly alike!

Scrapper was so muddy, he was covered from head to tail! He jumped up and down and ran in circles as I trotted over to him.

"Isn't this mud great?" Scrapper cheered. "I've been rolling in it all day! It feels so good. I even have mud in my ears. Oh, hey, wait a minute."

Scrapper stopped and stared at me. He walked right up to me and sniffed the air.

"Why aren't you muddy, buddy? And why do you smell like flowers? Did you—*GASP*—take a bath?"

"Yeah, but I played in the mud this morning," I said. "Now I'm looking for something. Something really important."

"Oh! Oh! Oh! Are you looking for buried treasure?" he asked.

I woofed *no*.

"Oh! Oh! Oh! Are you looking for more mud?" he asked.

I shook my head.

"Wait! Are you looking for the monster in the woods?" he asked as he shook off all the mud.

I answered no again, but I should tell you about Scrapper and the monster. He believed there was a monster living in the forest.

He swore he saw it once, and now he always hunts for it.

"No, I'm looking for my tag," I said.

Scrapper gave a big laugh. "That's no big deal. I lose my tag all the time. Just retrace your steps and check the places you went today."

I lowered my tail. "I already did that and still didn't find it."

"I bet you lost it at the house," Scrapper suggested. "You can look for it after we find the monster!"

Again with the monster!

"Could we do that another time?" I asked. "I really want to find my tag. It means a lot to me."

"Of course!" Scrapper wagged his tail. "Good luck!"

I wished Scrapper good luck with his monster too. I'm sure he'll find it one of these days.

King
and Diva

I walked back to the house and saw King and Diva waiting for me on the porch. They were always waiting for me on the porch.

"Stop! Who goes there?" King hissed.

"You know who it is," I said. "It's me, Bo. I live here, remember?"

"Hmmm," purred Diva. "That rings a bell. But the Bo who lives here has a tag with his name on it."

King and Diva slunk down the steps and stopped in front of me.

"And I don't see a tag on your collar," said Diva. "Maybe we should keep you out?"

I laughed nervously and tried to move past them. But the cats flicked their tails in my face and blocked the way to the porch.

"This isn't funny. You'd better let me pass," I said, "or—or I'll start barking!"

"Oh no! Not *barking*!" King and Diva pretended to be scared. "Oh, *please* don't bark! Whatever will we do? We're helpless against loud puppies who bark!"

They hissed and meowed a mean laugh.

"Come on, cats. Let me by. I need to find my tag," I said.

"Oh, right. Your tag," King said as he showed off his sharp teeth. "I heard something about your missing tag. What was it? I know! I heard it was all the way in the *up*-upstairs."

"Really?" I tried to keep my tail from wagging, but I couldn't help it. I was too excited. Dogs are not very good at hiding their feelings, and I may be the worst at it.

Still, the up-upstairs was a strange place for my tag to be.

"You aren't trying to fool me, are you?" I asked the barn cats, even though I kind of knew the answer.

"Oh, Bo," Diva said with a grin. "Why would we ever do that?"

9

The Up-Upstairs

The up-upstairs was what Imani and Wyatt called the attic. It's where the family keeps all their extra stuff, like clothes and chairs and decorations, and even beds.

We animals stay away from the up-upstairs. It's scary. But if my tag was up there, I had to be brave.

I climbed up to the porch, nudged the screen door open with my nose, and went inside.

After I bounded up to the second floor, I ran to the up-upstairs door at the end of the hallway.

It never closed all the way. Wyatt said that's because our house was so old.

I opened the door easily with my paw. It was dark, and the darkness surprised me because it was still day outside. Maybe light didn't exist in the up-upstairs?

With a gulp, I started up the steps.

They creaked slowly with my every move. It sounded like someone was following me . . . or *something*.

Suddenly I really hoped that Scrapper had caught his monster today and that it wasn't right behind me.

Just in case, I scrambled up the stairs and bumped right into a box full of winter clothes.

Then I whirled around to see if the monster was behind me. No one was there.

I took a deep breath and looked around the room. Even though the sun shone outside, the up-upstairs was cast in shadows. Most of the windows were blocked by stuff.

I could only make out the hulking shapes of boxes and old furniture. It was going to be impossible to find my tag in here . . . even if the barn cats were telling the truth.

I was about to give up when a small voice asked, "Can I help you?"

I tiptoed back toward the corner with my tail tucked under my tummy. I am not afraid to say that I am not a brave pup.

"Are you, um, the monster in the forest?" I forced myself to ask.

"Or are you a ghost that lives in the up-upstairs? Because if you are either of those things, I would like to leave."

"Don't be scared," said the voice. "I only want to help. We don't see many puppies up here."

"Well, I don't see many ghosts down there!" I whimpered.

"Ghosts? We aren't ghosts," the voice said. "We are spiders! Look up!"

I tipped my head back, and there was a spider, dangling from a thread just above me. It took every bit of courage not to run away.

"I—I'm Bo Davis," I said, "and I'm looking for my tag. See, it goes on my collar. It's shiny and heart-shaped. Have you seen it?"

The spider shook his tiny head. "I have not. But we will look for it."

I watched as more spiders hanging
from webs all over the ceiling flicked
their eyes around the room, searching.
Spiders have more eyes than me. That
was a lot of eyes looking for my tag.

"We do not see it here, I'm afraid,"
the spider said finally. "But let us send

a message to the other spiders in the house. Maybe they have seen it."

The spiders began to pluck at their webs, and I pricked my ears to listen. I could hear the quietest whisper of spider song. It sounded like a gentle breeze.

Then the spider above me smiled.
"We have found it downstairs, near
the bathroom!"

"Oh, wow, thank you, spiders!" I
said. "Thank you so much!"

I turned and bounded down the
steps. My heart was pounding. I was
so happy. Not only was my tag found
but I had also made new friends! Plus,
I had not met a monster or a ghost.
That's good news for a pup like me!

Home Is Where the Heart Is

I raced down the hall and slid right into the laundry hamper by the bathroom. I wish I could tell you this was the first time that had happened. But it wasn't. Somehow I slip and bump into things a lot.

The laundry basket tipped over, and a towel fell on the floor.

It was my towel from this morning! I sniffed it and could still smell the shampoo and mud. Those are two smells that go great together . . . especially if you are a dog!

Wyatt and Imani heard the crash and came running over.

"Oh, Bo, did you get muddy again?"
Wyatt asked.

I barked and rolled around on the
towel.

"No, he's clean as a whistle," said
Imani. "He seems to love that towel,
though."

Yes! The towel! Imani tried to pick it up, but I stepped on it with my paw.

"No, Bo. It's not playtime," she said. "And our towels are not toys."

Oh, sometimes I wish I could speak Human! It would make everyone's life so much easier!

Instead of shouting, *Hey, I think there's something UNDER the towel*, I got on my belly and rested my head on the towel. Then I gave Wyatt and Imani my biggest puppy dog eyes.

Wyatt bent down and picked up the towel. Something shiny fell out of the folds and bounced on the floor.

"Well, would you look at that!" Wyatt cheered. "You found your tag, Bo! Good dog!"

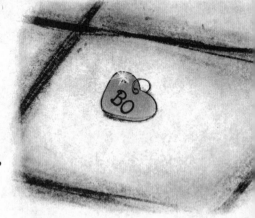

Wyatt slipped it back onto my collar while Imani found a tool to clamp its metal loop shut.

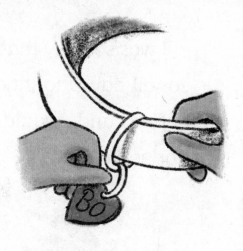

"There," she said, closing it. "Good as new. This tag should never fall off again."

With the mystery solved, we all went downstairs, where the kids poured some kibble into my bowl. Yum!

I was so busy that I had forgotten to eat all day. That had never happened before and would probably never happen again!

When I finished, I joined Wyatt and Imani on the sofa. They were reading books. I wished I could read books. It looked fun. But I wasn't going to learn that day.

I was dog-tired, which is like being a tired human times one hundred.

So I laid my head down on Imani's soft lap and closed my eyes. I'd had so many adventures, I think I earned a puppy nap. Besides, who knew what adventures awaited me tomorrow!

GOOD D🐾G
2

Raised in a Barn

CONTENTS

CHAPTER 1: COMET   129

CHAPTER 2: HORSING AROUND   141

CHAPTER 3: COACH BO   157

CHAPTER 4: FIRST THINGS FIRST   169

CHAPTER 5: HOLD YOUR HORSES   179

CHAPTER 6: BARN HAIR, DON'T CARE   189

CHAPTER 7: HORSE SHOW-AND-TELL   203

CHAPTER 8: DARN SQUIRRELS   213

CHAPTER 9: THE MAIN EVENT   223

CHAPTER 10: RAISED IN A BARN   239

Comet

The sky was a clear blue. Puffs of fluffy white clouds drifted above the Davis farm. The sunshine made the fur on my back feel nice and warm. Even the dirt smelled yummy, like leaves, flowers, and mud. I dug my paws deeper into the ground.

It was the perfect day for a race!

Comet came bounding out of the barn. Her horse legs still seemed a little bit too long for her horse body as she trotted over to me.

Comet is the new horse. She is Star and Grey's foal, and she thinks she's fast.

But I'm Bo Davis! Everyone knows I am the fastest animal around.

I can run faster than a chicken. I can run faster than a sheep. I can even run faster than my human brother and sister, Wyatt and Imani.

Plus, I can almost outrun the family truck, if it weren't for the fence I'm not supposed to cross.

That's why Comet and I needed to race: to prove once and for all who's the fastest on the Davis farm.

I greeted the young horse with a nod. "Morning, Comet."

"Hiya, Bo," she neighed cheerfully. "What a nice, sunny day!"

"It sure is," I said. "Are you ready to run?"

"You bet I am! And I'm going to win, too!" Comet said.

I woofed with a big puppy dog grin.

"Oh, Comet, I'm sorry, but I don't think so. I've been running since before you were born!"

Some of the sheep grazing in the field nearby lifted their heads and watched us. Zonks the pig glanced up from his trough and shuffled over.

"Wait, are you two racing?" he squealed. Then he hollered, "Hey, everyone! Bo and Comet are going to see who's faster—horses or dogs!"

Well, that was all the farm needed to hear. Soon all sorts of animals gathered around us.

Suddenly chickens, cows, sheep, and ducks were bickering about who they thought would win the race.

I could feel my heart beat a little bit quicker. We had an audience!

I tried to ignore everyone else and asked, "Where should we race to, Comet?"

She looked around the pasture, then lifted her nose toward the far end of the field.

"How about we race to that bale of hay down there?" Comet suggested.

"Okay," I agreed. "Where should we start?"

Before Comet could answer, Rufus the rooster strutted over.

Rufus was the head rooster, and where he went, animals paid attention.

He scratched a line in the dirt and clucked, "You will start here. Now take your marks, get set, and wait for my signal."

Horsing Around

As Comet and I stood next to each other, the rest of the farm animals lined the racecourse.

Comet arched her neck, then stuck it out straight and long. She was ready to dash.

I crouched low too and prepared to run as fast as I could.

Rufus counted down. "Okay. Three, two, one, cock-a-doodle-doo!"

I bounded out first, but I could feel Comet's hooves thumping the ground close behind me.

My legs stretched out as far as they could reach, and I moved through the air. I was almost floating, but I felt the grass tickle the pads of my paws.

The entire farm zipped by me. Or I zipped past it. Running like this makes dogs feel freer and happier than ever.

But Comet was still right behind me. She was fast for a foal!

I knew horses were good runners, but I didn't think she would be *this* speedy.

Then Comet wasn't behind me anymore. She was right next to me!

"Hi, Bo," she neighed.

Comet wasn't out of breath at all!
My tongue was hanging out, and I
was panting for air, but Comet looked
like she could run forever.

She smiled and said, "Bo, can you believe all the animals have come out to see us? And look at those pretty flowers!"

I didn't answer. I just watched that bale of hay coming closer and closer. But a loud squawk startled me.

A baby chick had wandered into the middle of our race! I bolted into the air and avoided a bad crash.

Those free-range chickens always get in the way!

Now Comet edged in front of me. Her legs pumped so fast that I knew the race was over. All I could do was watch her mane stream out behind her.

Then she slammed on the brakes and stopped!

This was my chance. I ran and ran
until I reached that hay bale first.

I hopped up on top of it, lifted my
nose in the air, and howled with joy.
"I'm so fast, no little foal could ever
beat me."

Nanny Sheep stepped out from behind the bale. She wore a frown and baaed in disappointment.

"Bo," she said, "you are behaving foolishly. A good sports-pup never teases other animals, whether you win or lose. I know Comet seems like a big horse, but she's still very young, and she has a lot to learn. Now go apologize."

I wasn't sure what Nanny Sheep meant by Comet still having a lot to learn. But I hung my head in shame. I hadn't meant to tease Comet or make her feel bad. Running just made me feel so good, and winning made me feel even better.

I found Comet sniffing the tall grass.
"Hey, Comet," I said. "I'm sorry for acting kind of mean when I won the race."

"It's okay, Bo," Comet said brightly. "Look what I found!"

With a toss of her head,
Comet nodded toward
a butterfly resting on a
flower. Its wings slowly
fluttered open and closed.

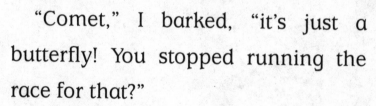

"Comet," I barked, "it's just a butterfly! You stopped running the race for that?"

I could not believe it!
Butterflies are pretty,
but a race is a race!
Comet just stared as
the butterfly lifted off
the flower and began to
flit around the pasture.

The young horse hopped after it, prancing around with her mouth wide open.

"Wow!" Comet said . . . until her mouth snapped shut and the butterfly was gone.

"Did you just eat the butterfly?!" I yelped. "We don't eat butterflies!"

Comet looked up at me guiltily, then opened her mouth.

The butterfly flew out quickly, shaking his head and grumbling under his breath about foals who need to learn their manners.

Gosh, maybe this is what Nanny Sheep meant when she said Comet still had a lot to learn.

Coach Bo

I took a long nap after the race. When I woke up later, I had lunch with Wyatt and Imani. Then my best puppy friend, Scrapper, came over for a visit.

We went out to the woods to search for his monster. Now, I've never seen a monster there, but Scrapper has.

And he's been trying to find it again ever since.

As we walked, I told Scrapper all about the race.

"A chick ducked into my path. Hey, the chick *ducked*. Get it?" I barked with a giggle.

Scrapper woofed. "That's funny, Bo!"

I kept on with my story. "Well, that chick slowed me down, and Comet pulled ahead. But then—"

Scrapper interrupted me. "Look, Bo! Did you see that over there?"

"See what?" I replied.

"That! Over there," he whispered. "Maybe it's a—"

We looked at each other and shouted together, "SQUIRREL!"

Sure enough, a squirrel was by the trees looking for nuts. We took off, and as soon as that squirrel saw us coming, he took off too. Right up a tree trunk and onto a branch that hung high over our heads.

Scrapper and I looked up and barked our heads off.

When we were sure the squirrel was gone, we continued on our way.

I sniffed the ground and kept a close eye out for more squirrels—and for Scrapper's monster, too.

"So, what happened, Bo?" Scrapper asked.

"Huh?" I said. "Oh, you mean with Comet? She stopped in the middle of the race to chase a—get this—a butterfly!"

"What? A butterfly?" Scrapper said wonderingly.

"Can you believe it?" I asked. "That poor foal doesn't know the first thing about being a horse!"

"Oooh, look over there!" Scrapper pushed his nose forward, and I could see a long shadow slipping between the trees.

"The monster!" we both said at the same time. We started to run toward it.

"Hey there, Mr. Monster, wait up!" Scrapper barked.

But it wasn't a monster. It was Imani and Wyatt.

"Hey, boy," Wyatt said, bending to scratch me behind my ears. He knows exactly where my favorite spot is.

"Are you and Scrapper hunting squirrels?" Imani leaned down to pat Scrapper.

I woofed to ask if they wanted to join, but I don't think they did. Humans just don't understand how important it is to chase squirrels.

"We have to go, but look, Bo," said Imani. She picked up a stick off the ground and tossed it through the air. "Fetch!"

Scrapper and I reached the stick at the same time and played a little game of tug-of-war until we got tired.

"You know," Scrapper said, "maybe Comet could be a great horse if she had the right teacher."

That gave me a bright idea!

"I think you're right, Scrapper," I told him. "Comet could use someone who knows about life on the farm."

"Yeah," Scrapper agreed. "Someone who is kind and honest and who will tell her when she makes a mistake."

I felt a big doggy grin spreading over my face. "I know the perfect teacher for Comet! Someone who knows all about the farm and who is always nice to her."

"Who's that?" asked Scrapper.

"Me!" I howled.

First Things First

I woke up early the next morning and went straight to the barn.

The first thing Comet needed to learn was that farm animals never sleep in.

"Wakey, wakey, Comet!" I called. "Time to rise and shine!"

Comet peeked her sleepy head out.

Then she yawned. "Bo? Are you in my dream?"

"You're not dreaming," I cheered. "It's morning, and you have horse lessons!"

"Horse lessons?" Comet asked.

I puffed out my chest. "Yep, you lucky foal! I'm going to teach you everything you need to know about being a horse. Now let's go eat."

Comet opened both eyes wide to stare at me. "What are you talking about?"

"I am talking about eating," I explained. "Humans eat in the house, and horses eat in the barn."

I walked over to the haystack and pulled a small clump of hay loose. "Here's some breakfast for you. Horses eat hay."

"I know how to eat, Bo," Comet huffed. "But thanks for the hay. I am pretty hungry."

She dipped her head and began to munch.

When she finished, I said, "Next, we take a morning walk. Because, um . . . well, because Mother Nature calls."

I headed out to the meadow, but Comet wasn't following me.

"Aren't you coming?" I asked.

"Um, Bo," she called from inside the barn, "is it safe to come out? Did you already, um, call on Mother Nature?"

I trotted back to the barn. I could

feel my cheeks getting warm under my fur. Comet sure wasn't making this any easier. "Oh, uh, yeah, I already went. But do you . . . ?"

Comet giggled. "I'm okay, but maybe we can just skip past this part of the lesson?"

Phew. What a relief.

"Yes, we can definitely skip past this and go on to the next lesson!" I said.

"What is it?" Comet asked.

"Uh, well . . . huh." I had no idea what should come next. "What do horses do all day?" I asked Comet.

"We like to take walks—*real* walks—to stretch our legs in the morning," Comet answered.

"A walk! Perfect!" I exclaimed. "Let's do that!"

5

Hold Your Horses

Comet and I headed into the delicious spring sunshine. As we walked, I pointed out some animals that were not from the farm.

"Look, Comet, see those evil guys with the big fluffy tails?" I asked.

A pair of chattering gray squirrels sat in the meadow.

They were probably planning something bad. I just knew it. You can't trust a squirrel.

"Those are squirrels," I explained. "We chase them, but they are really fast."

Oh, I could feel my legs itching to run after them.

"Okay. But why do you chase the squirrels?" Comet asked. "Have they done anything wrong?"

"Not yet," I replied quickly. "That's why we chase them. So they don't have a chance to do anything wrong."

Comet looked at me, then nodded slowly. "In that case, let's go!"

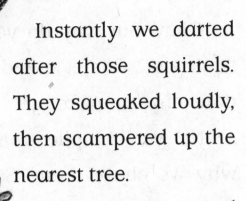

Instantly we darted after those squirrels. They squeaked loudly, then scampered up the nearest tree.

"That was some good squirrel chasing," I told Comet.

Suddenly a soft tweet came from above us. I looked up, and it was Blue the blue jay.

"Hi, Blue!" I called.

Blue waved his wing down to us.

"That's Blue," I explained to Comet. "He's a bird. Birds build nests in the

tree branches, and they mostly eat worms."

Comet neighed softly.

"Make sure you don't mix up birds and bats. Bats only come out at night," I told her. "They live in a bat house on top of the barn, and they're very helpful. They eat farm pests like moths and mosquitoes."

"I didn't know that," Comet said. "Do they eat flies? Those are the worst pests."

"Gosh, I don't know," I admitted.

Then I looked over at Comet and noticed her flicking her tail back and forth. She even swatted at her own back with it.

"What are you doing with your tail there?" I asked.

"I'm keeping the flies off me," she explained. "They're always bugging me and making my coat itch."

"Oh, I know how to keep the flies away," I said. "Look!"

I began rolling all over the ground.

"See how I roll back and forth in the dust?" I asked. "It feels good and scares the flies!"

"Let me try!" Comet said.

She lowered herself to the ground and began to roll. Then she started to giggle.

Pretty soon we were both laughing and rolling, kicking up small clouds of dust. Or maybe not so small.

Comet's parents, Star and Grey, trotted over and shouted, "Hold your horses, Comet!"

Uh-oh. I took one look at their long faces and knew that Comet's parents were not happy. Not one little bit.

6

Barn Hair, Don't Care

"What in the world are you doing?" Star whinnied.

"Bo is giving me horse lessons," Comet explained. "Rolling around on the ground is how horses keep flies away."

Star and Grey let out great big sighs.

"Comet," Grey said in a gentle voice, "horses don't roll on the ground to get rid of flies. We were worried you might be hurt!"

Then Star added, "It is very nice of Bo to help. But maybe he isn't the best animal to teach you about being a horse."

Hmm, I thought. "Star has a point. As a dog, maybe I don't really know how to be a horse."

Comet stood up, and her parents gasped. Comet's mane was a mess. It was tangled and dirty.

"Oh dear," said Star. "You were supposed to keep clean for the foal parade!"

"Parade?" I asked. "What parade?"

"There is a special parade for young foals at a local fair," said Grey. "Wyatt and Imani have worked so hard to groom Comet, getting her ready. But now they'll have to start all over again. Luckily, the parade isn't until tomorrow."

"So we have time," I woofed.

"Yes," said Star. "How about everyone comes into the barn, and we'll see what we can do about Comet's mane? Maybe Nanny Sheep knows a trick we can use."

As we all headed back to the barn, I saw two slim shadows slip inside first.

King and Diva. Those two barn cats always turn up when we least expect them.

"Oooh, Comet," Diva hissed from rafters at the top of the barn. "We love what you did for your hair."

"Yessss," King joined in. "That hairstyle is for the birds. Because it looks like a nest!"

Both cats cackled loudly and just about fell out of the rafters.

Comet hung her head and neighed softly. She seemed so sad, and those cats were not helping her feel any better.

"Hey!" I woofed at the cats. "You two had better cut it out!"

"Oh no, it's Bo, and he's barking mad," Diva meowed. "Can't Comet speak for herself? No, of course she can't! She's just a little baby horse!"

Before I knew what I was doing,
I jumped up the steps to the hayloft
and scared those cats. King and Diva
darted out the window with a hiss.

Then I heard a new sound. Comet
was crying.

I hopped down the steps and went to her side.

"Please don't let barn cats rain on your parade. They're just jealous," I told her. "You know, there's a saying all farm animals should learn: barn hair, don't care."

Comet sniffled. "What does that mean?"

"It means if you're working hard, then your hair will show it. But if your hair looks super neat, like those silly cats, well, it means you're hardly working at all."

"I like the sound of that," said Comet with a small whinny.

"Besides," I continued, "real farm animals don't care about how you look. They care about how you act."

Now there was a new neighing behind me. Star and Grey were in the doorway.

"You know, Bo, you are absolutely right. Maybe you do know something about horse life," Grey said.

"Now let's see what we can do about that mane," said Star. She trotted over to us and nuzzled Comet lovingly.

Horse
Show-and-Tell

The next day I woke up as soon as I heard Wyatt and Imani getting dressed. I knew they'd be working with Comet, and I wanted to go too.

I waited while they brushed their teeth and ate breakfast. When they finished, Imani scraped some eggs and bacon into my bowl. Yum!

As soon as the front door opened,
I headed straight for the barn. Imani
and Wyatt followed behind me.

The foal parade at the local fair
was that afternoon. So I knew this
morning would be all about getting
Comet ready. There would be lots of

grooming. I was excited for Comet and wanted to make sure no cats or squirrels bothered her.

Inside the barn, Wyatt pulled down a bridle. It was made of smooth brown leather and looked a lot like a leash.

When the kids showed me a leash, it meant we were going for a walk off the farm, which is one of my most favorite things!

I wanted to jump and howl with happiness, but I stopped myself. Young foals get nervous pretty easily, and I didn't want to bother Comet.

Wyatt gently stroked her nose and reminded her that the bridle would help Imani lead Comet in the parade. Comet whinnied softly and lowered her head.

Wyatt placed the bridle on her while Imani patted Comet's neck and whispered, "Good horse."

I felt my heart swell because Wyatt and Imani knew exactly how to treat Comet, gently and carefully. They probably knew how to care for every animal—whether it's a dog like me, a foal like Comet, or even squirrels.

That's why my humans are the best humans ever.

Next, Imani took a brush down from the shelf and told Comet that it was a soft dandy brush. She held it out so Comet could sniff the bristles. She even held it out for me to give it a sniff too.

I could smell Star's and Grey's and even Comet's scents. Their horsey smell was comforting. I gave a little woof, and Imani giggled.

Then she began to brush Comet from head to tail. She swept it in small, careful circles very slowly so she wouldn't startle Comet.

As I watched Imani brushing, I imagined the brush sweeping over my fur, and my back started to feel just a tiny bit itchy. Maybe tonight the kids would give me a back scratch.

"There," Imani said when she was done. "You look beautiful, Comet!"

And she really did. Her coat was so glossy, and her mane and tail were smooth and shiny.

"Okay, Comet, are you ready to practice our walk?" Imani asked.

Comet nodded and then followed Imani out of the barn.

Darn Squirrels

Wyatt walked to a fenced-in area and opened the gate.

The ground was covered in soft sand. I set one paw in it, not sure what it would feel like. The sand shifted under my pads and was almost as cool as mud.

Comet and Imani followed us.

Once they were inside, Wyatt closed the gate behind them. I looked up at Wyatt and tilted my head to the side.

"This is called the school," Wyatt explained. "We bring the horses here to practice riding. The fence keeps them safe, mostly by keeping other animals out. Horses can get nervous, especially

young ones like Comet. So we practice her parade walk in here first."

I wagged my tail. I loved it when Wyatt taught me new things.

We watched Imani lead Comet around the school. She guided the horse gently by the bridle.

After a few laps, Imani gave Comet
a carrot, which the foal gobbled up.

Yum. I was hungry too! I looked at
Wyatt and whimpered.

Wyatt laughed. "Sorry, Bo. Those
treats are for Comet."

I hung my head, but Wyatt quickly
cheered me up.

"Dogs don't eat horse treats, silly.
They need dog treats . . . like this one."
Then he tossed me a cookie bone!

OH BOY! Helping Comet was
delicious.

When practice was done, Imani led Comet out of the school and into the field. They walked back and forth around a water barrel and wove between a line of hay bales.

Comet was doing a great job. That is, until a squirrel showed up!

It bounded through the field just in front of Comet. I felt my legs get ready to spring after it, but Comet beat me to it.

As she pulled away to chase the squirrel, Imani held on to Comet's bridle with both hands and murmured calmly to her. Comet stopped pulling and obediently followed Imani back to the barn.

After Comet was back in her stall, Wyatt patted her nose and told her she did well.

But when we left to help Mom and Dad get the horse trailer, I heard Wyatt whisper to Imani, "I sure hope that doesn't happen at the parade!"

9

The Main Event

I dashed back to the barn. Suddenly I felt nervous.

"Comet, can I ask you something?" I said as I stood in front of her stall.

"Sure, Bo," she said. "You know you can ask me anything."

"Why did you chase that squirrel?" I asked.

"Because you taught me to," Comet answered. "I did a good job, didn't I? I scared it away."

Oh no. I pawed at the straw on the floor. Now I felt terrible.

"Um, Comet," I whimpered, "I don't think I'm such a good horse teacher.

I know a lot about the farm. I know all about being a dog. But I don't know much about being a horse. You should forget everything I taught you."

I turned to leave, but Star and Grey were standing behind me. I hadn't heard them come in.

"Bo, you may not know about being a horse, but you know a lot about being a good friend," Star said. "And that's exactly what Comet needs."

Grey nodded, then faced Comet. "And you, young foal—we saw you walking with the kids outside. Your mother and I have never been more proud of you. You did a terrific job, and we know you are going to do great at the parade today."

The family nuzzled noses.

Now I felt warm and fuzzy inside, just as Darnell and Jennica, my human dad and mom, joined us in the barn.

It was time for the parade. They led Comet out to the trailer.

As I watched her walk away, I wished more than anything that I could go with Comet. Then Jennica came back to the barn, and she was holding . . . my leash! I was going to go with Comet!

It was very crowded at the fairground. People were everywhere, but I could still walk easily through the park with my family.

There were so many new smells swirling all around me. I sniffed salty, buttery popcorn; yummy, meaty hamburgers; and sweet, grassy hay! The scents were all mixed together, dancing in the air.

Imani and Wyatt went on a few rides. And there was an art show with pictures hung up in a small gallery outdoors.

One painting looked just like a giant bone. Maybe it *was* a giant bone!

I was about to take a test bite when a loud voice announced, "Ladies and gentlemen, girls and boys, it's time for the Foal Show!"

Jennica and Darnell led me over to the show area. It looked like the school back at our farm.

We watched as, one by one, a line of kids walked their foals around the ring. Parents stood outside the fence clapping happily. All the foals looked so proud as they trotted by, though a few were a bit startled when they spotted me.

Finally, Imani and Comet came out.
Comet's mane was smooth and silky,
her coat glistened in the sunlight, and
all the dust had been brushed from
her legs.

As she walked around the ring, I kept a close lookout for squirrels, but luckily none appeared. I gave a happy woof as Comet walked by me.

Comet grinned a horsey grin and winked as she went past. My puppy heart beat so fast. I couldn't wait to tell all the animals back on the farm about it.

Raised in a Barn

Back home, I helped Imani and Wyatt get Comet down from the trailer and take her back to the stall.

They both patted her on the neck and fished out some carrots for her.

"You did such a good job today, Comet," Imani said. "You get the rest of the week off!"

When the kids left, I stayed behind.
My tail wagged fast because I was
bursting with pride and excitement.

"Guess what, Comet!" I shouted. "Some of the other horses got so surprised when they saw me that they forgot where they were! Just like what happened when you saw that squirrel earlier. But not you. You did great!"

Comet laughed and said, "I guess horses just don't like surprises so much."

Now it was my turn to laugh. "Hmm, then I don't think you're going to like this!"

I darted out of the stall, and Comet trotted after me.

"SURPRISE!" everyone shouted.
All the animals on the farm gathered
together to celebrate Comet's big day.

Comet told everyone about the foal parade, and I told everyone about the fair.

Then Star and Grey told us about the first show they walked in when they were foals. That was where they met and fell in love!

Then, farm animals being farm animals, everyone had a story to share. And as I listened to my friends, that warm and fuzzy feeling began to fill me up again.

I was one lucky pup to be raised in a barn like this.

GOOD D🐾G

3

Herd You Loud and Clear

CONTENTS

CHAPTER 1: PUFFS — 251

CHAPTER 2: THE BAA BAA SHOP — 267

CHAPTER 3: ROCK AND ROLL — 283

CHAPTER 4: NANNY SHEEP — 297

CHAPTER 5: I THINK I CAN — 305

CHAPTER 6: FLUFFY FLOCK — 315

CHAPTER 7: MONSTER HUNT — 327

CHAPTER 8: A LITTLE HELP — 337

CHAPTER 9: BOOGIE PUP — 347

CHAPTER 10: HERD YOU LOUD AND CLEAR — 357

Puffs

How in the world do sheep stay so fluffy—no matter what they do?

Whenever I spend the day playing outside in the field, my fur gets tangled and wild. If I take a nap lying against a tree, my fur is smooshed flat and totally dirty when I wake up.

And I don't even want to tell you what happens when I roll around in the barn.

But sheep are different from dogs. No matter what they do, they are always puffy. Their wool seems to stay bouncy and cheerful like a cloud all the time.

There is just one problem. Even though they look super soft, sheep do *not* like to be used as pillows. I learned that the hard way.

There is something that sheep *do* love: playing hide-and-seek. And that was what we were doing on a sunny afternoon.

My buddy Puffs was hiding. I was seeking.

Puffs is a very nice sheep, and he's a really good friend. But he's not the best at playing hide-and-seek.

When he's the seeker, he almost
always forgets that we are playing a
game. If something catches his eye,
he'll wander over to check it out and
forget to come find me!

And if he is the one hiding, well, let's just say he doesn't always remember how fluffy and white he is . . . and it's hard enough to find good hiding spots in an open green field.

If Puffs hides
behind a tree—I
found you!

If Puffs hides
behind a big hay
bale—I found you!

If Puffs hides
behind another
sheep—well, that's a
little bit trickier, but
still—I found you!

Today Puffs tried hiding next to the cows grazing in the field.

"Found *MOO*!" I yelled, and the cows laughed so hard, I think a little milk came out of their noses.

"Aw, that's no fair!" Puffs said. "You're too good at this game, Bo! You always find me. Hmm, are you sure you're not cheating?"

"No way!" I told Puffs. "Dogs never cheat. It's impossible. We're just not built that way."

"Then how in the world did you find me?" the young sheep asked. "This hiding spot was perfect!"

I didn't have the heart to tell him that while cows are bigger than sheep, they have spots, and they are not fluffy.

You see, cows and sheep do not look anything alike, but they don't smell alike either. I mean, they are totally different animals. So when a sheep tries to blend in with a herd of cows to fool a dog like me, it doesn't work. They stick out like, well, a woolly sheep.

"Hmm," I said, thinking, "maybe I am just a lucky hide-and-seeker."

Puffs nodded. "Yeah, that must be it. Because I know this was a really good hiding spot."

As we headed back toward the flock of sheep, Puffs listed some other games we could play.

"Have you ever played tag?" he asked me.

"Yep, that's fun," I answered.

"What about freeze tag?" he tried.

"Yep, I've played that, too," I said.

"Oh! What about sheep frog?" Puffs asked.

"Nope," I said. "Wait. Um, is that like leapfrog, where you hop over your friends?"

"Yes, but in sheep frog, you hop over sheep friends," said Puffs. "But it sounds like you've played it. Gosh, Bo. Is there *any* game you aren't good at?"

I thought for a minute, then said, "I'm sure there is, but we will have to find it later. I have a few more pup chores to do before dinner tonight. See you tomorrow?"

"Okay," said Puffs. "But I'm going to find a game that you've never ever played. I promise!"

I chuckled as he bounded over to his sheep friends. If anyone could find a game like that, it would probably be Puffs.

The Baa Baa Shop

The next morning Rufus the rooster woke everybody up with an amazingly loud cock-a-doodle-doo.

I got up right away, all ready to get my day started. My human family was a different story. It was very hard for them to wake up. Everyone seemed to move in the slowest slow motion.

Hurry, hurry! I wanted to bark. *The day is ready to greet us!*

But I tried my best to be patient.
That can be very hard for a dog.
After everyone ate a good breakfast,
we were finally ready to go.

It was going to be a big day. The sheep's wool had grown too full, so Darnell needed me to help herd them so he could give the sheep haircuts. Actually, Darnell called it getting shorn, but the sheep liked to call it getting a haircut.

But there were other things we had to do before trimming the sheep.

We began the morning with our everyday farmyard chores. First, we fed Zonks and the other pigs. They were happy to see us, but even happier to see their trough filled with slop.

Then we brought feed to the horses.

Comet, the foal, said she was starving
when we came. And I believed her!
She took huge, gobbling bites of her
breakfast.

Star and Grey were her parents. They were probably hungry too, but they were kind and let Comet eat first. When she was all done, Darnell chuckled and poured some more feed for Star and Grey.

Next we fed the cows and stopped by the chicken pen to toss seeds and kernels of corn.

Cheep cheep cheep, the chicks chirped as they scooted around the yard pecking at the seeds. You know, when those little chicks are hungry, they sure move fast.

At last we made it out to the field, where the sheep were scattered here and there.

"Bo, do you think you can herd these fluffy guys?" Darnell asked.

I barked *yes!*

"Good," he said. "Now go round up those sheep and bring them back to the barn. It's time to open the Baa Baa Shop!"

The Baa Baa Shop was what Darnell called the barn when he was shearing wool from the sheep. Wyatt and Imani thought it was a really funny name, but I didn't get the joke. Humans can be silly like that.

I bolted toward the sheep with Darnell's instructions in mind. It felt great to run through the field in the morning. There was just a little bit of dew left on the grass to cool off my belly. Plus, the sun began to pop up over the trees and warm my back. I was proud to be a good dog who could help out around the farm.

I ran to the first sheep and asked
him to head to the barn, because it
was time for a haircut. He nodded his
head and began to walk toward the
barn. I was off to a good start!

After gathering a few more sheep, I realized I hadn't seen Puffs. I stopped and looked for a second, but I couldn't find him anywhere. Where could that little lamb have gotten to? Did he finally score a good hiding place?

I dashed around the field barking his name.

But as I ran, I noticed that some of the sheep I had sent to the Baa Baa Shop were not doing as I had asked.

So this time, I walked each of them over to the barn, one by one. But every few steps, they stopped to eat another bite of grass. They were moving so slowly. They dragged their feet. They forgot what they were doing.

A few of them even asked if I would carry them up to the barn because it was too far away and they were so hot from all their wool.

All I could do was roll my eyes. What was going on with these lazy sheep? Didn't any of them want to get a haircut?

Rock
and Roll

After leading several sheep to the barn, I went looking for Puffs again. Hmm, sheep don't get great at hiding overnight, so where had he gone?

When I finally found him, I couldn't believe I hadn't spotted him sooner. He was standing on a rock at the far end of the field.

"Hey, Puffs," I said. "It's time to come down. Darnell is giving out haircuts."

But Puffs just shook his head playfully. He had a spark in his eye, and I could tell that he wanted to turn this rock into another one of his silly games.

"No!" he cried. "Not until you come up here and catch me, Bo!"

"I've got work to do, Puffs," I said. "Now's not a good time to play."

"You hear that, world?" Puffs yelled out. "Bo Davis is too scared to climb a little old rock!"

Now he'd done it. It was time to teach him a lesson. I put my front paws on the rock and tried to pull myself up, but I slipped. I tried it again using my claws to get a grip, but the cold, hard stone was too slick.

No one was happier about this than Puffs. He giggled and baaed with delight as I slipped and slid around the base of the rock.

"Stop laughing, Puffs," I said.

But he didn't. Instead, he called other sheep over to watch, and they started laughing at me too.

I looked at my paws. If they wouldn't work, I needed a new plan to get Puffs off that rock. I needed to try something different. So I barked really loudly. I mean, this bark was so loud that it echoed through the field. I hoped it would scare Puffs, but he didn't budge.

Next I tried swatting Puffs with my tail, but that didn't work either.

"Wow, Bo! You really can't do it, can you?" Puffs said. "Maybe we should start calling you No-Go-Bo!"

All the sheep watching gasped at Puffs's new nickname for me, and I felt an angry tingling in the back of my neck. Puffs had turned a silly game into something mean. And I do not like mean things.

As the young sheep laughed on top of his rock, I backed up farther and farther. Then I took a running start and launched myself up onto that rock!

And it worked!

Actually, maybe it worked a little too well. I made it onto the rock, but I couldn't get my footing, so I slammed into Puffs. The two of us rolled off the rock and tumbled into the cool grass below.

My head was still spinning when
a very un-puffy sheep walked over.
The other sheep noticed him too and
wanted to know where he had gotten
his hair cut.

The shorn sheep explained that Darnell was giving trims at the Baa Baa Shop—which is exactly what I had been trying to tell everyone! I began to feel very frustrated.

Then Puffs and his friends headed to the barn without saying good-bye. Instead, they were all laughing about how No-Go-Bo couldn't even climb a silly rock.

Had Puffs finally found a game that I wasn't good at?

Nanny Sheep

It's hard to not be good at something. As a puppy, I've always been lucky. There were so many things I was good at from the very first time I tried them.

Like escaping my gate! Wyatt and Imani love to tell me about my first night at home. I was supposed to stay in a gated area downstairs.

I liked it until everyone else went upstairs, and I was all alone.

Did I cry and whine about it? Well, maybe a little. But then I used my paws to open the gate and found the perfect place to go to sleep for the night. A cozy spot on the rug right between Wyatt's and Imani's bedrooms. Then I didn't feel lonely anymore.

And there were lots of other things
I was good at: racing, digging, playing
fetch, and tug-of-war.

But I wasn't very good at climbing rocks. Or herding sheep. And I'm supposed to be a sheepdog! At least, that's what Darnell told me. But herding was hard, especially with these stubborn sheep.

I rolled over in the grass and lowered my head. What was I doing wrong?

"Good morning, Bo," came a familiar and comforting voice. It was Nanny Sheep. She was standing on Puffs's rock looking down at me.

"Aww, even you can climb the rock." I whimpered. "What's wrong with me?"

Nanny Sheep hopped down off the rock and stood close to me.

"Bo, sheep have a very different kind of foot from what dogs have," she explained. "We have hooves, which make it easier for sheep to climb on uneven surfaces. You have paws, which can be good for climbing, but climbing rocks is not as easy as walking on the ground."

I smiled. "That makes me feel a little better. But it's not just rock climbing.

I really need to work on my herding skills. I feel like I'm letting Darnell down."

"I can help you with herding, Bo," Nanny Sheep offered. "Why don't you come back after lunch?"

Oh, that got my tail wagging like wild. Not only was Nanny Sheep going to teach me how to herd, but it was also lunchtime! I thanked her and ran back to the house, where a bowl of chow had my name on it.

5

I Think
I Can

After lunch I was in a pretty good mood again, but unfortunately that didn't last long.

Stretched out lazily on the porch were those darn barn cats, King and Diva.

I tried to sneak by them, but those cats were waiting for me.

"Aww, poor Bo," said Diva, with an unkind grin. "I heard the news. Did the great big puppy have trouble climbing the teeny tiny rock?"

I knew I shouldn't let them get to me, but I couldn't help it. I barked and barked, which set them running and brought Jennica out of the house.

"Quiet, Bo!" she scolded. "Those barn cats aren't bothering anyone, so you let them be!"

I hung my head low and stared at those mean cats as they slunk to the edge of the porch. Then I went on my way.

Luckily it was a beautiful day. The sun had slipped behind the clouds, and there was a light breeze that cooled the air.

Nanny Sheep was waiting for me by the rock.

"Oh no, are we climbing the rock again?" I asked, looking around. I definitely did not want an audience.

"No." Nanny Sheep nudged a red ball toward me with her nose. It was Wyatt and Imani's kickball.

I loved chasing that thing around. My tail started wagging at the sight of it.

"Are we going to play fetch?" I asked excitedly.

"No, Bo," said Nanny Sheep. "You are going to learn how to herd sheep."

I was confused. "Do I need a ball to herd sheep?"

That made Nanny Sheep laugh. "No, the ball will help you *learn* how to herd. I am going to kick the ball. You must chase it and nudge the ball with your nose to keep it moving toward the barn. If the ball rolls away from your path, you must give it a little push to make it go in the right direction."

"That seems easy enough," I said.

But it wasn't! First, Nanny Sheep kicked the ball away from the barn. I ran after it and gave it a nudge, but I did it too hard. The ball went flying in another direction away from the barn again.

After a few tries I started to get the hang of it. I wove from side to side, making sure the ball kept rolling in a nearly straight line until we reached the barn.

When I got there, Nanny Sheep was waiting.

"You took too long," she said. "Try it again. Guide the ball down to the rock and return here as fast as you can."

I ran back and forth with the ball over and over. At the end of each run Nanny Sheep would say one word: "Again."

So I ran again and again . . . and again.

Finally, after an hour, Nanny Sheep
said, "Bo, I think you are ready to herd
some real sheep now."

Fluffy Flock

Junior was the biggest, fluffiest sheep of the flock.

He towered next to Nanny Sheep and looked down at me.

"Okay, Bo. Your mission is to guide Junior to the barn," Nanny Sheep told me.

"With the ball?" I asked.

She laughed. "Oh, silly pup. You're going to herd sheep instead of the ball this time!"

I leaned closer to Nanny Sheep and whispered, "But I don't know how, remember?"

"Yes, you do," she said. "You herd the sheep the same way you handled the ball. If Junior steps out of line, you guide him back into place."

I nodded, then looked at Junior. "Okay, let's go to the barn."

And just like that he walked . . . in the wrong direction. I darted to one side of him and nudged him back on track. To my amazement, it worked!

Until he stopped to eat some grass.
I nudged him again, but Junior kept
chomping away. With a sheep this big,
I figured there was only one way to get
his attention.

I barked my command this time. "GET TO THE BARN NOW, MISTER!"

Now, I'm not a yeller, but that made Junior march! He hiked all the way up the hill and into the barn.

I ran back to Nanny Sheep and cheered. "I did it! I did it!"

Nanny Sheep smiled and said, "Now try herding two sheep."

So I did. Then all of a sudden, I was herding three, four, and five sheep!

When I was done, Nanny Sheep smiled at me and said, "Job well done, little pup!"

"Thanks for your help," I said. "I wish Puffs were here to see this. Where is he, anyway?"

Nanny Sheep looked around. "I'm sure he's off playing somewhere. That Puffs always has some kind of game hidden in his wool."

"You've got that right," I said as I turned to leave. "Thanks again!"

"It was my pleasure, Bo," she said.

Then I had a thought. "Hey, Nanny Sheep. I don't suppose you have any advice for how to handle two pesky barn cats, do you?"

Nanny Sheep shook her head. "Oh, there's no cure for those two cats."

That made me laugh because she was probably right!

As I was heading home, my friend Scrapper raced out of the woods to surprise me.

"Bo! Bo! Hey, Bo!" He yipped and sped over so fast that instead of stopping, he tumbled right past me.

"What's the rush?" I asked.

"Monster! I found a monster in the forest!" he barked excitedly. "Follow me!"

Well, what else was a pup to do? A monster in the forest? Now that was something I had to see for myself.

Monster Hunt

The woods were a fun place to go— even if you were searching for a monster. I mean, just look at all the squirrels to chase!

Plus, there were so many smells to sniff. Plants, trees, and dirt, just to start. There were plenty of animal scents that I had never smelled too.

Maybe one of those smells belonged
to Scrapper's monster, which he is
always looking for!

This time Scrapper had spotted the
monster on a ledge near the river, so
we headed that way.

As I jogged beside him, I asked him what the monster looked like.

"It was big . . . but also little," said Scrapper. "And it was fluffy, and it climbed up the ledge really fast."

So, it was a big, little monster who could climb fast and was fluffy? This sounded very interesting.

"Did you talk to it?" I asked Scrapper.

He looked surprised. "No way, Bo! It's a monster! Monsters don't make friends. They make trouble."

I thought about that, and it made me feel a little bit sad. Even monsters deserve friends.

"Well, we don't know that *this* monster wants to make trouble," I explained. "We should try to say hello. That's what good neighbors do, after all."

We reached the river, and Scrapper pointed his nose toward the cliff next to a waterfall.

When I looked up, I actually saw something fluffy on the rocks, but it definitely wasn't a monster.

A Little
Help

"Puffs!" I shouted, because I knew that fluffy white hair anywhere.

Somehow that sneaky little sheep had wandered into the forest to climb up the rocky cliffside.

"This had better not be one of your silly games!" I called. "Come down and let's go home!"

But Puffs didn't move. He was frozen in place. I could tell from the look in his eyes that something was wrong. He was scared.

Then I realized what was going on.
Puffs was stuck!

A few other young sheep stepped
out from between the trees.

"Bo!" they said. "Thank goodness!
We were playing hide-and-seek, and
Puffs found the perfect hiding spot. But
now he can't get down!"

Oh boy, I wanted to growl at the lambs, but I stayed calm.

"You all know that sheep aren't supposed to be in the forest ever," I reminded them.

"We know, Bo! And we're sorry!" they said. "If you get Puffs down, then we promise we'll never come back into the forest again!"

I studied the rock wall, wishing that Nanny Sheep could have given me climbing lessons as well as herding lessons.

The wall was steep, but I had to help Puffs. He was my friend. Plus, he was a sheep, and it was my job to keep the sheep safe. After all, I was a sheepdog!

I carefully pawed the rocks and took one slow step at a time.

When all four of my paws were balanced on the rocks, I stopped. The surface didn't feel right under the pads of my paws. The ground was too slippery and uneven. How in the world would I ever do this?

Suddenly I wasn't alone on the
rocks. Scrapper scrambled right
past me.

"Do you need some help, Bo?" he
asked.

I was very surprised to see him. "How did you do that?" I asked.

"Do what? Oh, you mean climb on the rocks?" he said. Scrapper quickly ran around in a little circle. "It's super easy if you know the secret!"

Boogie
Pup

Scrapper skipped down next to me like it was the easiest thing in the world. "The first step to climbing," he explained, "is to remember that walking on rocks is not like walking on the ground."

"Well, gosh, I already figured that out!" I said.

347

"Great! Then you're ready for the next step." Scrapper woofed. "The secret to climbing rocks is to make it fun and *not* scary."

I looked up at Puffs. He seemed a long way away. Nothing seemed fun or not scary about climbing up there.

"Umm, I don't really know how to do that," I told him.

"Well, I like to dance," Scrapper said.

"And how is that supposed to help me get to Puffs?" I asked.

Scrapper's tail wagged wildly. "Easy! Dancing makes me happy, so when I climb the rocks, I pretend I'm dancing over them. I mean, I don't go fast, but putting a little shimmy in my step helps me keep my balance."

I watched as Scrapper did a little jig over the rocks. I could see that the way his paws skipped over the rocks helped him keep his footing.

"Now you try," Scrapper called.

I *do* like to dance—not as much as I like running. But whenever I dance, I feel happy. So I gave a little shake of my tail and took a quick step forward. And another step and another, and soon I was hopping and bopping up the rocks.

Finally I reached Puffs, and the little
sheep was so happy to see me, he
baaed. "Wow, Bo, that was amazing! Is
there anything you're not good at?"

"Well, I wasn't good at climbing rocks at first," I admitted. "But with good friends to help me, maybe anything is possible. Now let's get down . . . and I don't mean dance."

I taught Puffs how to *cha-cha-cha* to the bottom of the rocks. We sang, *"One, two, cha-cha-cha,"* until we reached solid ground.

Puffs hung his head as the other sheep flocked to him.

"Are you okay, Puffs?" I asked.

"Gee, Bo. I'm sorry for laughing at you earlier today," the young sheep apologized. "I would have been stuck there forever if you hadn't shown up. Can you ever forgive me?"

"Hey, it's okay, buddy," I said. "Now let's get you back to the farm before anyone notices you wandered off."

Herd You
Loud and Clear

Sheep are very smart creatures, but they're also very curious. This is why they need to be herded from place to place. And let me tell you, herding sheep through the woods is not easy!

Even with Puffs and Scrapper trying to help, I had to work hard to keep the other sheep together.

As we wound our way between the trees, one little sheep wandered off to check out a log. He licked it and made a funny face. I guess it didn't taste good. I bounded behind him and nudged him back to the other sheep.

Then a chipmunk skittered across the path. It startled two sheep at the front of the line. I guess they'd never seen a chipmunk before, because they started to follow it. I dashed after them and gave them a gentle push back to the flock.

We continued along until there was a loud tap-tap-tapping sound as a shower of acorns fell from an oak tree to the forest floor. The acorn attack made all of us jump—even me, although I knew it was just a squirrel up in the branches. Darn squirrels!

Scrapper ran up to me and said, "Hey, Bo, what if *that* was the monster?"

I woofed *no*, but the little sheep I was
leading got scared once they heard the
word "monster."

They scattered in all directions.

"Thanks, Scrapper," I huffed.

Then I ran back and forth, nudging one sheep after the other into one flock.

When we finally left the woods behind us and got back to the farm, Nanny Sheep was waiting for us. And she wasn't alone.

Comet was there with Star and Grey, Zonks, and a bunch of other sheep with very short haircuts.

Everyone cheered as I guided the sheep through the field.

"I knew you could do it, Bo," Nanny Sheep said with a big smile.

"Thanks, Nanny Sheep," I said. "It turns out that with some help from my friends, I can do a lot of things I didn't think I could."

"Speaking of which," said Scrapper, coming over, "do you think you can teach me to herd sheep too?"

"Sure!" I told him. "It starts with chasing one of these."

I nudged the red kickball toward Scrapper. And as he chased after it, I had a hunch he would make a great herding dog too.

GOOD D🐾G
4

Fireworks Night

CONTENTS

CHAPTER 1: SCRAPPER — 373

CHAPTER 2: SUMMER DAYS — 385

CHAPTER 3: SUMMER NIGHTS — 399

CHAPTER 4: MEAN CATS KITTEN AROUND — 411

CHAPTER 5: WHAT'S A FIREWORK? — 423

CHAPTER 6: ALL THE SMELLS — 437

CHAPTER 7: COLOR SKY — 451

CHAPTER 8: SCARY OR VERY SCARY — 461

CHAPTER 9: BRAVE PUPPY — 475

CHAPTER 10: FIREWORKS NIGHT — 485

Scrapper

You might not think that puppies are the kind of animals who are interested in secret forts, but guess what? We totally are!

This is Scrapper. He's my best dog friend. He lives one house over from the Davis farm.

There's a forest in between our homes, and we love to play there. But not today. Today we were playing at Scrapper's house.

Scrapper has three humans in his family. There's Tom and Rey and their son, Hank. Hank's a really great kid, but more importantly, he's an amazing ball-thrower.

Humans might not understand why dogs like to play fetch so much. But honestly, I can't see how it's so different from two people playing catch.

Only, fetch is better! You get to run all over the place and catch the ball—or stick or Frisbee—in your mouth. Then you get to chew and slobber all over it!

What's not to love about that? Humans should try it sometime.

Plus, if it weren't for fetch, Scrapper and I would have never discovered our secret dog fort!

You see, we were playing a special game of fetch. Hank had a brand-new bouncy ball. How bouncy was it? It was faster and bouncier than any ball I'd ever seen.

On Hank's first toss, that ball flew deep into the woods, and Scrapper and I chased after it.

That ball rolled past rocks, flew off roots, and sprang over fallen tree trunks.

When it finally slowed down, guess where it had landed? Right in front of a small, gray, bushy-tailed squirrel!

Now, what was a dog supposed to do when he had to choose between a ball and a squirrel?

I froze. Scrapper paused. But that squirrel sure knew what to do.

He kicked the ball as hard as he could with both his feet and sent it flying even deeper into the forest.

And then he took off running, hopping away as fast as he could go.

Scrapper and I looked at each other. There was only one choice.

I mean, we could chase squirrels anytime—there were so many of them in the woods. But there was only one wonderful mega bouncy ball that we knew of. And we had to catch it!

Panting and feeling the wind whooshing through our fur, we dashed between trees and leaped over logs searching for that ball.

Finally, Scrapper and I skidded to a stop when we found it nestled in a bed of moss to the side of a pile of fallen trees. I went after the ball, but Scrapper was looking at something else.

Summer Days

I turned to see what Scrapper had found. He was sniffing at the base of the tree.

Suddenly, he stood on his hind legs and pushed on one of the tree trunks with his front paw.

"Waaa ah ooo oooing?" I asked.

But Scrapper couldn't understand me.

It's hard to talk with a ball gripped between your teeth.

I set the ball down and tried again. "What are you doing?"

"I'm discovering!" Scrapper yipped excitedly.

"Discovering what?" I asked. "A stack of old wood?"

I could not figure out why Scrapper's tail was wagging so happily. Clearly, I was missing something.

Scrapper poked his head into a narrow gap between two tree trunks. Then the rest of him followed and he disappeared! Oh, no! That tree ate my friend!

I pounced against that tree with my paws and barked as loud as I could!

"Calm down, Bo!" a voice echoed from inside the tree.

Hmm, that voice sounded a lot like Scrapper, I thought.

Then my best friend burst from between the trees with a humongous smile on his face.

"Bo! You have to see this! It's our new puppy fort!" he shouted. "Come with me and check it out!"

Phew! So I guess trees don't eat dogs. I felt very happy about that . . . and a little silly for thinking they might.

Scrapper waved me over with a nod of his head and darted back inside the fort.

First I picked up the ball because you never know what evil plots those squirrels might be hatching. Then I stepped through to the dark shadows between the trees.

It was cool inside the circle of trees, which felt nice. Summer days at the farm could be awfully hot, even in the shade.

A little bit of light shined through the roof formed by tree branches and leaves above us. This meant we still could easily see all around us.

"It's great, right?" Scrapper asked. "We can use this as our secret hideout while looking for *you-know-what*!"

I wish I could say that Scrapper wanted to search for squirrels. But I knew he was talking about keeping watch for his monster.

Scrapper was certain that there was a monster living in this forest. He even thought he had seen it before. I wasn't so sure, but Scrapper was my best friend. And best friends help each other out, even if it means hunting monsters.

"That sounds like a plan," I said, "but we better get back before Hank doesn't want to play fetch anymore."

"Good idea," Scrapper agreed. "But first let's mark our fort so we know how to find it tonight!"

Do you know how dogs leave their mark? Well, let me tell you—it isn't pretty.

Summer
Nights

Summer days on the farm were hot, but summer nights were nice and cool.

After dinner, I stepped outside and felt the breeze ruffling my fur. It was soft and comforting, like an old friend.

The sky glowed purple and orange as the sun began to dip behind the trees. I headed for the forest to meet Scrapper.

He was waiting for me in front of the fort with a bag.

"First order of dog business, this place needs a name," Scrapper said. "I vote for Camp Monster-Finder."

I thought that was a pretty good name. It said what it was.

"Oh, and I brought stuff that monsters like," Scrapper told me.

He nuzzled open the bag and flipped it upside down. There was a yummy-looking bone, a comic book that I guessed belonged to Hank, some glow-in-the-dark toys, and a monster mask.

"Won't you get in trouble for taking these things?" I asked.

"Oh, I'll bring them back later," said Scrapper. "Besides, Hank never plays with these anymore. This comic book has been under his bed for weeks. And he hasn't worn the mask in a year."

I sniffed at the mask. It was pretty weird-looking. "Do you think the mask might scare away the monster?"

"Bo," Scrapper said with a chuckle. "You just don't understand monsters the way I do. They are very curious creatures. If they see another monster, they're going to want to come over to see what it's doing."

"But what about the comic book? Can monsters even read?" I asked doubtfully.

Scrapper thought about that one.

"They can look at the pictures," he answered. "Plus, monsters need toys that glow to play with, because they come out at night. And I brought the bone in case the monster gets hungry. We all know a bone is great to chew on."

Hmmm. Scrapper was making a lot of sense!

We scattered the supplies on the ground and in the bushes outside the fort, and then we went to wait inside.

The night was quiet, and it was getting late. Even the squirrels were asleep by now. Just as my eyelids were starting to grow heavy, it happened.

There was a very loud, whistling SCREECH followed by a thundering BOOM that echoed above us.

Scrapper and I jumped from the fort and looked up just in time to see a shower of sizzling lights in the sky.

They snapped and popped and fizzed
their way right down toward us.

"It's the MONSTER!" Scrapper yelled.
And that was all we needed to know.
It was time to go, go, go!

Mean Cats
Kitten Around

Running through a dark forest at night with an angry monster exploding above us was not fun. Not fun at all.

But Scrapper and I were fast. We hightailed it to my house, then skidded to a sudden stop on the front path.

Those pesky barn cats, King and Diva, were lying on the porch. It was like they had been waiting for us.

"What's the rush, little pups?" Diva hissed with a wicked grin. "You look so frightened! Is there a big scary squirrel chasing you?"

"This is no time for jokes, Diva!" Scrapper howled. "There is a monster after us!"

Another burst of light exploded in the sky with a loud bang.

"See!" I yelped.

But those barn cats didn't flinch or
look scared at all. They just rolled over
onto their backs and started laughing
their whiskers off.

"Hey, it's not funny!" Scrapper said.

"Oh, you silly pups," said King.
"Those lights in the
sky aren't a monster."

"Huh. What are they,
then?" I asked.

King sat up and started to clean his paws. He licked between each sharp claw. "Those are just stars," he said.

"I've never seen stars that do that," said Scrapper.

"Pups, don't you know stars explode when they're angry?" Diva asked. "And the stars must be very angry with you, Scrapper!"

He looked terrified, and his tail drooped between his legs.

"But why? What did I do wrong?" he cried.

That's when Imani and Wyatt, my human sister and brother, stepped out onto the porch. The screen door slammed shut behind them with a loud crack that startled the cats.

Diva and King hopped to their feet and slunk away faster than a pup could snatch a scrap of food that fell under the dinner table.

417

Unfortunately, the loud noise also scared Scrapper off. He darted away before I could even say good-bye.

"Bo! I'm so glad you're here," said Imani as she waved me over.

I bounded up the steps and leaped into her arms. I was really scared, and it felt good to be held when I was frightened.

419

Wyatt gave me a soft pat too. "Poor Bo, you are shaking! Are you scared? I bet it was the fireworks. They can be upsetting with all that noise."

"Don't worry, Bo," Imani said, planting a kiss on my head. "You're safe. This is just a little practice for the big show tomorrow night.

We'll make sure we stay with you when the real fireworks go off."

Imani carried me inside and set me down. Now I was wondering what in the world they were talking about.

5

What's a Firework?

The next morning my human parents, Darnell and Jennica, were busy in the kitchen.

I could smell all kinds of good food cooking: biscuits, cookies, beans, corn, potatoes. I also spied piles of hot dogs and plates of uncooked hamburger patties in the fridge.

This was way more food than the Davis family usually ate. I wondered what was going on.

I joined Wyatt and Imani for chore time.

While they fed the pigs, I asked my good friend Zonks if today was a special farm day or something.

Zonks thought for a moment, then said, "I don't think so. But there is one animal who would know."

He didn't even have to say another word. I knew just the animal to ask.

I trotted out to the field and found Nanny Sheep talking to a flock of lambs. I sat down next to them in the grass.

"My dear lamb friends," Nanny Sheep began. "And my puppy friend, too. Tonight is a very special night for the humans. This year the Davis family is having a party for their friends. They will eat lots of food, and they will be happy and very noisy. And then, when it gets dark, there will be a fireworks show."

Oh, I sat up even straighter and raised my paw. I had heard that word before!

"Fireworks? What are those?" I barked.

"Fireworks are special lights that humans send up into the night sky," Nanny Sheep explained. "The lights glow and spin and spark and shine. But they also make a very loud sound.

You may have heard or seen the fireworks last night."

Several of the lambs looked around at one another and nodded.

One young lamb jumped to his feet and baaed. "I heard them, and I was so scared!"

I woofed in agreement. I had felt the same way last night!

Another lamb puffed out his wool. "I was afraid too!"

The lambs all began nodding and baaing. I guess Scrapper and I weren't the only animals freaked out by the fireworks.

Nanny Sheep gently hushed us. "Yes, my young ones, fireworks can certainly be surprising, especially when we are used to the stars shining quietly in the sky. But for humans this

is a very special night, and they like
to celebrate. So, just remember that
although fireworks are noisy, they
are supposed to be fun and make
everyone smile."

Oh boy, I felt so much better now! Leave it to Nanny Sheep to calm everybody down and explain exactly what needed explaining.

I couldn't wait to tell Scrapper. He didn't have to feel sad or scared anymore either. Those barn cats were just teasing him last night.

For now, though, I could hear Wyatt calling me back home.

A pup's work is never done.

6

All the Smells

Later that day the party started. First a few people arrived, and then more and more trickled into the yard. I had never seen so many cars and trucks parked at the farm.

And with every new visitor came a new tray of food! And believe me, it smelled yummy!

I imagined what it would be like if all those humans were bringing all that tasty food just for me. That was a yummy tummy daydream!

Finally, a truck that I knew all too well pulled through the gates. It was Scrapper's family! I ran over to greet them with happy barks, but when the doors opened, only Hank and his parents stepped out. Where was Scrapper?

I must have looked really confused, because Hank leaned down and patted my head.

"Hi, Bo," he said. "Are you looking for Scrapper?"

I gave a yip and spun around in a circle.

Hank let out a laugh. "Aww, I'm so sorry, Bo. Scrapper stayed home. Something scared him pretty bad last night. It was probably the fireworks, but just in case, we didn't want him to come to the party and get scared.

So we're just going to be here until the fireworks begin. Then we'll go home to make sure he's all right."

I was impressed. Hank was such a thoughtful dog owner and an all-around great human. I gave him a lick, then led him over to the backyard, where the party was in full swing.

Being a dog at a party is *never* boring. There is so much to see, and lots to hear, of course. And then there are *all the smells*.

Sure, there's always amazing food, but the people at a party have lots of different scents too! Some wear perfume, some, um . . . don't. Some

humans smell like candy or cookies or meat. Others can smell like coffee— mainly just the grown-up humans. No matter what, they all smell interesting.

As the party went on, the sky grew darker. Luckily, the Davis family had outside lights set up. When they switched on, it was magical.

The other great thing about this party was that people ate outside. And outside eating means they use paper plates. And do you know what happens when people eat using paper plates? Food spills on the ground.

And guess what else? Humans almost never eat food that falls on the ground. And when they're outdoors, they usually don't even pick it up. Do you know who does? DOGS!

And I was the only dog around.

I found chips. I found vegetables and cookies and cake crumbs. I found hot dog buns. I even found half a hot dog! What a night!

I was so busy sniffing around that I found a smell I wasn't expecting at all hiding under a picnic table. It was Scrapper!

"Hey!" I cried. "What are you doing here? Hank said you were staying at home."

"Do I look like the kind of dog who stays at home, Bo?" he said. "No. No, I don't. I'm a party dog. And do you know what I am here to do, Bo?"

"Um . . . party?" I guessed.

"You know it!" he cheered. "Now, let's find the man in the brown boots. He's carrying a baby who keeps throwing food on the ground. It's amazing!"

I laughed. Scrapper was such a smart dog when it came to finding food scraps. Maybe that was why they called him Scrapper?

We found the man in the brown boots who was holding the baby, and sure enough, that kid didn't want to eat anything! Which of course meant that Scrapper and I ate everything.

With our bellies full, I didn't think
the night could get any better.
And I was right.

Color
Sky

"Okay, friends, it's fireworks time!" Darnell announced excitedly.

The crowd sat on blankets in the lawn, and everybody looked up in the sky.

Everyone except Hank's family. I saw their truck driving back to their house.

"Fireworks? What are those?" asked Scrapper. "They sound fancy."

Oh, no! We were so busy hunting for food that I'd forgotten to let Scrapper know what Nanny Sheep had told us about fireworks!

I tried to warn him, but it was too late.

The night sky exploded with color. Whistles and booms echoed across the countryside, with bangs so loud I thought the sky was cracking open.

It didn't matter that I knew we were safe.
Scrapper didn't! He whined loudly and tore
off into the woods.

I chased after him, but Scrapper has

always been much faster than I am.
And the dark did not make things
easier. I ran as quickly as I could,
trying to catch up to him.

"Scrapper!" I shouted between the blasts of the fireworks. "Scrapper, hey, it's okay!"

The noise was so loud. There was no way he would ever hear me. I panted, squinting my eyes to try to see through the trees.

Another blast of fireworks filled the air. Even I had a hard time believing everything was okay when the sky was busy with such loud thunder and lights.

When I made it to Scrapper's house,
I scratched at the door with my paw
and barked loudly.

Hank opened the door immediately.
He looked very worried.

"Bo! Have you seen Scrapper? He isn't here!" Hank sounded even more upset than he looked.

Uh-oh. If Scrapper wasn't home, where was he?

Scary or Very Scary

Another firework lit up the night and sizzled over the forest.

Hey, the forest! Suddenly I knew exactly where to find my best pup friend. I left Hank and charged into the trees.

The forest was a little scary at night, but I reminded myself that there was nothing to worry about.

I headed straight for our fort. Well, as straight as one could go in a forest at night.

Scrapper *had* to be at Camp Monster-Finder. It was the only answer!

As the fireworks whizzed and boomed brightly above the trees, the shadows in the forest lit up briefly before darkness quickly swept back over them.

The lights played tricks on my eyes.
Every stump turned into Scrapper's
monster. Tree branches looked like
claws reaching toward me.

Okay, I was wrong. The forest was actually VERY scary at night. But I was on a mission, and I couldn't back out. I woofed and ran faster.

Then I stopped. I didn't want to be
afraid anymore, so I closed my eyes
and tried to use my nose to pick up
Scrapper's scent.

I took a deep breath. The whole forest smelled like rotten eggs for some reason. Maybe it had something to do with the fireworks?

Finally, I caught Scrapper's scent and ran toward our fort!

Oh, I was so happy when I found it that I howled with joy. Then I saw something glowing in a bush next to the fort. They looked like eyes . . . and they were watching me!

"Scrapper?" I whispered. "Scrapper, is that you?"

The glowing eyes blinked at the sound of my voice. Then they started moving toward me. My heart raced, but I was not going anywhere without my friend.

I don't know what came over me, but I jumped up on my hind legs and let out the deepest bark I could. Luckily, a firework went off at the same time, and it made my bark go BOOM!

And it worked! The glowing eyes scrambled all around like scaredy little squirrels. That's because they were squirrels! Squirrels playing with the glow toys Scrapper had brought to the fort.

I let out a great big sigh of relief.

That's when something else jumped out of the fort. It had the body of a dog with the terrible, horrible head of . . . a MONSTER!

Brave Puppy

"Woof, woof, woof, woof!" the monster barked at the squirrels. They dropped the toys and raced off into the forest faster than a squirrel had ever run.

Please be a nice monster! Please be a nice monster! was all I could think.

The beast stopped barking and turned to face me.

As its big, ugly head swiveled in my direction, I felt my doggy heart pound. Then the monster spoke. "Are you okay, Bo?"

I knew that voice! It was Scrapper! He shook his head, and the monster mask flew off. I've never been so happy to see Scrapper's big grin.

"Did you see those silly squirrels? I really fooled them!" Scrapper boasted.

"You fooled me, too!" I screamed.

"Aw, I'm sorry about that," said Scrapper. He looked up at the sky, suddenly nervous. "Hey, uh, we should go before the stars get angry again."

"The stars?" I said. "Oh, those aren't stars. They're fireworks, and have I got news for you!"

First I told Scrapper that he should never, ever trust the word of a barn cat. They were only interested in making trouble. Then I told him that fireworks weren't supposed to be scary.

"They're flashes of light that the humans make to celebrate. Tonight is some sort of big deal for humans," I explained. "So to celebrate it, they bring color at night."

"Really?" Scrapper asked.

"Really!" I said. "All the humans are back at my farm watching the sky and cheering."

"Gosh, Bo," said Scrapper as he looked at the ground with his tail drooping. "You must think I'm the silliest scaredy-cat pup ever."

I shook my head. "No way, Scrapper! Even during the scary fireworks, you left the fort to rescue me from those squirrels. I think that makes you one of the bravest pups I know! And my very best friend."

Scrapper wagged his tail and said,
"You know what, Bo? Now that I think
about it, you're right! Plus, you came
looking for me and stood up to those
squirrels—which means you're my
very best friend too."

I held out my paw and said, "Best friends forever?"

Scrapper slapped his paw down on mine. "Totally! Now let's go back to my house and watch the rest of the angry stars before they go back to sleep."

Fireworks
Night

When Hank saw Scrapper, he wrapped him up in a great big hug!

Then the three of us sat on the porch watching the rest of the fireworks show. Hank even gave us some cookie treats that tasted like chicken. Yum!

That was our first Fireworks Night, but it wouldn't be the last.

In fact, there were lots more, and let me tell you—we always ate well! One time a whole pie fell on the ground, and we got to eat the entire thing. Okay, maybe the pie had a little help falling down to the ground. But no one was any the wiser, and it was worth it.

Another time, King and Diva tried to play a practical joke on us, but it totally backfired.

See, they wanted Scrapper and me to stand under a table so they could dump a bowl full of punch on us. But when a firework exploded in the sky, it scared those cats so bad, they lost their balance. And do you know where they landed? Right in the punch bowl!

You should have seen it! They looked so funny, soaked to their barn-cat bones. Scrapper and I laughed so hard, our sides started to hurt!

Oh, and once, Hank had a sleepover with Wyatt, which meant Scrapper got to spend the night too! We stayed awake almost all night long, watching the fireworks, then listening to Hank and Wyatt tell ghost stories.

Plus, they shared their snacks with us. Scrapper and I even got to try some marshmallows when the boys made hot cocoa. How cool is that?

So now Scrapper and I look forward to Fireworks Night every year. But I will never ever forget our very first Fireworks Night. Because that's the night we became best friends forever.

Here's a peek at Bo's next big adventure!

GOOD D🐾G

The Swimming Hole

Every farm has a big tree.

You know, a huge one with wide limbs perfect for human kids to climb. One that you can't miss.

Sometimes the tree is next to the barn. Sometimes it's in front of the house.

An excerpt from *The Swimming Hole*

The big tree on our farm is in the middle of the field. And during the hottest days of summer, everyone gathers there.

Why? you might ask. Because the big tree gives the absolute coolest, best shade.

Every animal on the farm needs shade on hot summer days. The cats stay in the barn, horses stay in their stalls, and pigs stay in the mud—if they are lucky enough to find a pool of mud.

But when it is so hot that it feels like the sun is tapping you on the back, the best place to be is under the big tree.

An excerpt from *The Swimming Hole*

All the animals meet there, and it's like a party. Well, it's more like a slumber party, because everybody likes to close their eyes and enjoy the sweet breeze.

One sunny day, a young bird perched in the branches of the big tree and began singing.

I liked his song. It went like this: "Tweetly tweet tweet, sweetly tweet tweet twee."

Billy the goat, on the other hand, did not like the song. He did not like it at all.

An excerpt from *The Swimming Hole*

So Billy did what any goat would do. He climbed into the big tree. I'd never seen that before—it was pretty neat!

The bird didn't think it was so cool, though. He flew away with a squawk and left Billy up in the branches all by himself.

An excerpt from *The Swimming Hole*

GOOD D🐾G

Hungry for more adventures?

Visit Bo and his friends at
simonandschusterpublishing.com/readandlearn